Pashmina

NIDHI CHANANI

Pashmina

First Second
New York

For Nick,
Lil Moon
& Leela

You know, Shakti misses Shiva, so she asks the gods for advice.

They say either choose sadness or choose to meditate on the word om. Shakti chooses to meditate.

She repeats om over and over loudly. It begins to rain. She doesn't notice.

Eventually the rainwater makes an ocean. She's under it, but still she meditates.

I don't see the connection.

It's a choice, Mom!

Choose to be calm. How come you can use these stories, but I can't?

Shakti didn't have to ride in the car with a teenager.

Hey, what about this?

It can be a wordless panel.

Yeah! I like it.

You're much better at this than me.

Whatcha drawing, Thrift Store?

Pri, you need to enter this *OC Register* comics contest.

Oh cool!

It says they get over a thousand entries.

You could be the winner!

I don't think so...

Thanks anyway.

Thrift Store.

9

Yeah, since I don't have kids, I read articles and see if you fit the formula.

That's really nerdy.

Want to practice driving this weekend? We can put your mom in the car.

She might have a heart attack!

I taught your mom to drive years and years ago. I'm sure it's hard for her to see you grow up.

You and Auntie Deepa should come to the movies on Saturday.

Only if you drive.

You have to convince my mom.

Done!

12

God is a part of life, Priyanka.

I've prayed to Shakti my whole entire life. She always listens.

How was school? Did you take the bus?

No, Uncle Jatin dropped me.

Jatin and Deepa
are like family.
They knew you when
you were a baby.

I'm happy you have
a good relation with them.
Your uncle Jatin enjoys
telling you about India.

He's always been
like that. They helped
me when I first arrived.
Did you know—

Did Uncle Jatin
know my dad?

Want to see *Sholay* on the big screen Saturday?

You always change the subject.

It has your favorite star, Amitabh, in it!

Sure, whatever.

sigh

BOOF!

Stupid closet!

Shakti, I don't ask for much. Please...

Please don't take Uncle Jatin away from me.

He doesn't NEED a baby.

This Shakti stuff doesn't work, Mom.

What do you mean?

Maybe you should've stayed there.

With my dad.

Life isn't simple anywhere, Priyanka.

When I came to the US, I thought it would be better. Certain things are good, like it's very clean. But not enough respect here. As for your dad...

...that subject is permanently closed.

Dear Nimisha-di,
I know you haven't replied to my previous letters but I am your sister and I miss you... All of us miss you here. I will keep writing to you for as long as I can. The news here...

Is that Mom?

I wonder what it's doing here.

Trust us, it's not important.

Are you sure?

Of course!

It's samosa time!

WHOOSH

Beta, I'm home!

Hi, Mom.

Hi.

How are you?

Fine. How come you never talk about your sister?

Your Meena Mausi?

Yeah, were you close?

Why this sudden interest in your Meena Mausi?

Mom! Just answer!

We were close. It's harder to be a girl in India than you think.

Want Chai?

49

She was teased a lot because she wore my old clothes. I saved my pocket money for weeks to buy her new salwars.

MOOOOOM!

What?

You know girls get teased for their clothes here, too, right?

Maybe... but in India it's different.

I couldn't go.

I know it's sad but your Uncle Jatin and Auntie Deepa need our support.

Sometimes we have to do the hard things.

FWWUMP

What happened?

I can't see!

Say good-bye to those date killers, Priyanka Das!

It's Pri. Whoa, how strange.

Oh my gulab jamun, you're in for a treat!

Huh?

Follow me.

Is that thread?

Hey, Pri!

Feeling okay?

Not really . . .

Give it time.

I didn't tell you. I found an old suitcase in our hall closet. It was strange because it smelled like samosas.

You need help with your samosa obsession!

Ha ha, probably.

Did you find a stash of samosas inside the suitcase?

Never mind.

What?! Wait, which one?

The "Gym Tree"!

Anyway, it won!

You won!

Huh? What did I win?

$500, and they're publishing it!

Way to go!

All the information is in here. Congrats!

Wow. Thanks, Mr. Perry.

Well, Kanta, what next?

It's your choice.

What do you want to see?

I guess I want to see more.

Done!

1/ CLAP CLAP

How's my award-winning cartoonist?

Uhh, okay.

Working on the next great American comic?

Not really.

Gotta go.

Ja!
Get out!

P*HAT**!

Wait!

What do you want?

Leave it, Priyanka. We have much to do.

Why don't you want me to see it?

WHAT IS IT?

Priyanka!

You spend a lot of time in your room.

So?

Is that against the law?

No, I am just worried about you.

I went to Hawa Mahal when I was younger.

They built it that way so women could see out. They weren't allowed to show their face in public.

Ew, really? But it's so beautiful . . .

hawa mahal

I was thinking if you have questions, I can answer them. You don't need to go to India.

Mom.

I can't explain it. I feel like I need to go. I don't know why you won't let me go.

I KNOW there's beauty there.

India is a poor, dirty place.

It does have beauty. More than here, but all that beauty isn't what it seems.

Wow.

Where's the shadow?

Don't worry. She's gone.

Isn't the Taj amazing?

She?

I feel like she wanted to tell me something.

Why don't you let me talk to her?

Bhabi, the mattar parathas were great.

Thanks, Jatin bhai.

I'm happy you have time away from the hospital.

Ready for chai?

Maybe later. Why are you so quiet, Priyanka?

Priyanka is very mad on me. She wants to go to India and I said no.

Why India?

I feel like it will help me understand.

India isn't a safe place to go alone, Priyanka.

Your mom is right.

Sorry, I know you're dealing with baby Shilpa.

Yeah, we miss you.

I know it's no fun, but you can come see her with us.

I always ask her to come. Maybe it's too much for her.

We understand. If you went to India, we would miss you more.

Never mind.

Let's change the topic. Chai?

You know, your auntie and uncle are going through a lot.

You were so quiet and moody.

You're really pushing me.

What? I didn't want to talk. That's all. Am I **required** to talk?

Sometimes I don't know what to do with you.

You **don't come** to the hospital.

You have these **crazy ideas.**

Going to India is **crazy?**

It's not that easy. I don't want you to go. It's **not** safe or happy like you **imagine** it is.

82

Didi? Hello? It's Meena. I know we haven't talked in a long time, but for some reason I couldn't stop thinking about you today.

I had to call you. How are you?

Even though she's my younger sister and she didn't understand, I feel that I failed her.

From the stories you tell, it seems like she cares about you.

Yeah.

Never mind that.

Do you still want to visit India?

Is this a trick question?

No, beta.

OF COURSE! YES!

Meena is three months pregnant. She's scared.

I will **never return** to India.

Plus my hands are full with your uncle, your auntie, and Shilpa . . .

But I thought since you were asking . . .

Meena Mausi is expecting you.

Thank you, Mommy!

Ha ha ha! Thank your Meena Mausi.

Wow! I will see India AND meet your sister!

If your mausi hadn't called, I would never send you there.

Where's my favorite pen?

okay, enough clothes. If you need more, get them washed there.

What else?

Found it!

It's hard to let you go, beta. Promise you'll call whenever you can? I'll call Mausi, too.

Yeah, Mom. I will call.

Welcome to Netaji Subhas Chandra Bose International Airport.

Priyanka, beta!

You are Nimisha-di's duplicate!

No need for this, beta.

Jai Shakti.

The kids in Jadav Pur are very bright. When I started teaching years ago, I thought no one would care.

But they want to learn.

Girls especially!

You're a teacher?

What has your mom told you?

How is she?

That day I couldn't rest until we spoke.

I wish she had come, too.

Not much. Fine.

She hates India.

Sorry, beta. No elevator here.

Whew!

First time in our home, na?

You're a little Lakshmi, Priyanka.

You can call me Pri.

Huh? Did you know Shakti is the goddess of energy and power? She is like the mother to us all.

NOO!

SPLOSH

Mausi, maybe this sounds crazy. I haven't told anyone but this is my mom's shawl, and when I put it on, it took me to India. Not this India ... the India like tour books—full of palaces, tigers, and yummy food. There are two guides, Kanta and Mayur. They are my friends. I wanted to see them again, so I put the shawl on ... maybe it doesn't work because I'm already in India?

I don't understand. Why?

WOOOO

So the shawl works for you but not me. I don't understand what's happening.

What is this pashmina?

Where did you find it?

In my mom's suitcase.

It's from here. I mean India.

It's Assam silk. Exceptional handiwork. Sualkuchi silks maybe? They're famous for this kind of work.

Can we go there?!

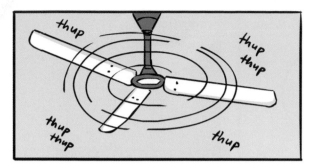
thup
thup thup
thup thup
thup

OWAAH

Not a good idea. You're four months pregnant now.

Sahib, it's your niece's first request. Why not? Maan kartha hai. Nagpur is safe.

Why Nagpur? Something about her father?

No. She hasn't talked about him. She isn't comfortable yet, na?

I don't like it. Tour Kolkata, even Delhi. No Nagpur.

If Delhi, why not Nagpur? I can take her where she wants to go.

Meena, I don't like you teaching in the slums and I don't like this Nagpur business.

I said no.

Can we go slower?

Yes, madam. This is slow.

PUTUR PUTURR

ISSHH!

Victoria Memorial is very nice.

It looks like stuff in the US. I thought we could see a palace.

British monuments are part of India. I thought you'd like it.

Idea! Let's visit Jadav Pur— you can meet the girls I used to teach.

Used to?

Your mausa-ji agreed after many requests. But when I became pregnant, he refused.

Oh! They will love to meet you and practice their English!

A leaf plate!

Oh my god, this dosa is so good.

Oops.

I've never been anywhere like that. It was so sad.

Sad? Why? They are learning and that will change their lives, Priyanka.

Do not look at the dirt. Look at the people.

But I can't help feeling sad for the girls. My mom told me about the poverty... but it's another thing to see it.

But they are being educated. That is what matters.

I've shown you the up and down of Kolkata.

Now what? Cinema?

Maybe we can go home first? I'm pretty tired.

Of course, beta.

Hello, Sahib.

Hello, hello! How was your day, Priyanka?

I took her to New Market, Victoria, and . . . Jadav Pur.

What? Jadav Pur! Why would Priyanka want to see that?

Mausa-ji, I chose to visit Jadav Pur. It was eye-opening.

I don't know why you came, if you're in some identity crisis. Next time, it's best to go where I suggest.

She's **fine**, Sahib. No crisis. We had a good time but she's **tired**, so it's time to take a rest.

Phuu

Is Mausa-ji **mad** at me?

No, no, beta. That's just his way of **talking**. Don't mind it.

-hmmm

PRIMARY SCHOOL

1. Sunila Shah   16. Ria Mitra
2. Neera Patel   17. Shaila Singh
3. Kiran Das   18. Pallavi Rali
4. Anjali Kaur   19. Nisha Kaur
5. Swati Rao   20. Sajal Khan
6. Riddhiti   21. Madhusuda
7. Noor Falah   22. Sangeeta Jai
8. Shazia Ali   23. Sheetal Kana
9. kamala G   24. Laxmi Jana
10. Gita Mehta   25. Faheema C
11. Praveena   26. Rama Laal
                    27. Radha Gan

DHUM!

I saw my daughter trying to teach in the slums.

Like you?

We must go to Nagpur, to Sualkuchi silks.

But Mausa-ji...

Never mind that. It's my choice. We are going.

Let's go. Tomorrow.

So...
Did you know
my father?

No, I didn't want
to know him.

What do you
mean?

What has
your mom told
you about
Rahul?

That's his
name?

You didn't
know? If your
mom hasn't said,
I don't know
if I should.

Do you know
why your mom left
India?

No, why?

Mausi, please? My mom will never tell me. How can I understand if I don't know?

You should know the truth. Rahul was set to marry Nimisha-di and convinced her to visit him... before their marriage. Then she found she was pregnant.

It was awful.

I guess he didn't want to marry her after all or he didn't want the responsibility of a child.

He canceled the wedding.

HE canceled the wedding...?

His family knew that if Nimisha-di stayed in the area it would bring his family dishonor. They had money and power. Rahul married another girl. They offered to arrange for your mom to leave.

Our Uncle Maneesh had contacts in the US... I believe you know them, Jatin and Deepa?

It was very scary for us all. I remember sending your mom off at the airport...

Because of me.

I can't believe it. I had so many ideas of who my dad might be...

I never thought about why my mom didn't say. Because he's terrible. He caused her so much pain.

That's why she never told me—she knew I'd blame myself. And I kept asking her...

God.

This is hard, beta. Don't take any blame on yourself.

It's because of Rahul that I've been afraid of your mausa-ji. I was scared to **choose** myself.

Your mom left because she was trying to **protect** you. I wish she came back. We knew she would have you there, but we thought she would **return** someday.

And all these years I wondered. What a waste.

How did she get the shawl?

I don't know, beta. I don't remember seeing her with it.

You know your mom was your age . . .

When she left? Yeah.

Pardon, bhabi? Do you recognize this shawl?

Nahi, ji.

Do you know who made this?

No, ma'am.

Na.

Excuse me, do you know who embroidered this pashmina?

Beautiful handiwork.

Ha ji, this is the work of Rohini.

Rohini was the fastest weaver in AP, she worked in a factory in Warangal. You cannot mistake these patterns.

Where's Warangal?

Take us to Warangal Silks.

Closed, madam.

It's up ahead, there. I can feel it.

huuh

SILKS · PAS

It's destroyed.

Look!

SILKS · PASH

Can I have the pashmina?

Wait out here.

DHAMAK!

Kanta!

Mayur!

FWOSH

Hello, Priyanka.

It was 1944 in Warangal. The factory was the only job for women for miles.

Rohini! Did you hear the factory is moving?

You will come with me to the new factory. You are the fastest, after all.

Ji.

And my personal favorite.

I didn't want to be the fastest or the favorite. I wanted another life.

tug

HEH HEH

138

I went into the flames. It was my task and my choice.

I felt protected by lord Shakti.

I worked without rest for days. Weaving the glowing thread.

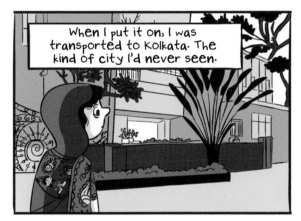

When I put it on, I was transported to Kolkata. The kind of city I'd never seen.

Rohini-di!

Rohini, can you take Pavani and get some subjis?

Yes, memsahib.

Rohini! Call me Reena. You're like family!

I saw a possible future free of factory work. I saw my life full of joy and in my control.

Beta, are you okay?

Shakti?

I was called here? Rohini Mitra? The factory and the pashmina and lord Shakti... golden thread...

Who's Rohini Mitra? Familiar name... What did you see exactly?

Take your time.

You should keep this.

I don't know . . .

Pass it on to your daughter.

If you can't find a use for the pashmina, I promise I'll come back for it.

I tried to call but it seemed like you were having a lot of fun with Mausi.

Yeah, Mausi and I had a good time. She reminds me of you.

Everyone used to say that we were like twins.

And your mausa-ji? I never met him...

He's kind of weird. I spent most of my time with Mausi.

You think your mommy is stupid? Ha ha. I knew you found it.

I left it with Mausi.

When your father decided not to marry me, I didn't know what to do. Your Nani Pavani had a pashmina she got from her nanny, Rohini. The night the engagement was canceled, I wrapped it around my shoulders.

What happened?

I saw America. It was amazing and shiny. It was full of fancy technology and beautiful buildings. So clean . . .

But that America exists only in the Pashmina. Reality is very different!

I KNOW what you mean! Ha ha.

That vision made me ask my parents to find a way to send me to America. I would never have considered it before.

ahh

Life with you would've been impossible in India. Here I can be independent. I made the right choice.

I'm sorry, Mom.

It's not your fault.

NEVER think that.

Mausi said the same.

But I am sorry. For everything. I am so sorry I bothered you about that awful man and that I fought with you.

Oh yeah!

Mausi sent these petha for you. She said it's probably been years since you had them.

My favorite! I bought these from the corner sweet shop anytime I had pocket money.

Well, now anytime I need petha I will just send you to India!

That's a long way to go to satisfy a sweet tooth.

Not for me. That's why I have you!

I do want to go back and meet the baby...

PLAYA LN
RANCHO I

Hi, beta!

Shilpa! Say, "Priyanka didi"!

We missed you, Priyanka.

I missed you all, too.

RING
RING

Newspaper
- theme
- column

Hey, you two! Welcome back.

How was your break? Do anything exciting you want to share?

I wrote my own comic book!

Glossary

Note: Indian children are taught to address elders as Auntie or Uncle as a form of respect. From taxi drivers to parents' friends, we refer to all Indian elders as Uncle or Auntie.

Beta: Son or daughter, often adults will address children who aren't blood related with this term as a sign of endearment

Bhabi: Sister-in-law, also symbolic term used to address friend's wife

Didi: Sister, often shortened to "di"

Diwali: The festival of lights, celebrated by lighting candles and fireworks to chase away the dark and invite light into your home for the new year—arguably one of the best holidays ever

Dosa: A large, savory Indian crepe best enjoyed with heaps of coconut chutney

Garam: Warm

Holi: Festival celebrating the arrival of spring, celebrators will play and throw colored powder and colored water on each other, accompanied by singing and dancing

Ja: Go

Ji: A gender-neutral honorific suffix, similar to the Japanese "-san"

Kya: What

Laddu/Sandesh/Jelabi/Halwa/Petha: Various Indian sweets

Mausa: Uncle, formally your mother's brother-in-law

Mausi: Auntie, formally your mother's sister

Memsahib: Madam

Mithai: Sweets

NRI: Non-resident Indian

Sabji: Vegetable

Sahib: Mister, some women address their husbands as Sahib as a sign of respect

Salwar: Indian women's dress

Samosa: A delicious triangular pastry filled with potatoes and spices

Acknowledgments

To Mark Siegel, for taking a chance on a new voice and guiding me through each phase with kindness and support. To say I couldn't have done it without you is undeniably true.

To my agent, Judy Hansen, for being my career guide and fierce advocate. Thank you for always believing that I'm worth more than the first offer.

To my mom, who taught me how to read and then allowed me to do so everywhere, including the dinner table. We both know *Pashmina* is truly about making peace with our white hair.

To my hubbahubba, Nick, it's due to your steadfast support that I became an artist and made this book. You are the reason my dreams have come true.

To my friend editors Lyla Warren and Rhode Montijo, your feedback and loving eye helped me in the crucial development phase. Your friendship and willingness to discuss story ad nauseam are wonderful gifts.

To Bernie, my sweet mother-in-law, your unreserved faith in me helps when I'm doubtful. Your help with Leela was paramount to completing this book.

To Nickole Caimol, who assisted with tone pages and prepared all the files for printing. You are my sounding board, wise beyond your years, and I am eager to see what you create next.

To my friends: Many of you appear in the backgrounds of this book. Some of your names are hidden in marquees and lists. Others, I trolled your Facebook photos and drew you, so thank you for unknowingly being my models.

Pashmina was not made alone, I relied heavily on my team of friends. To Roberto Chicas, Sunila Rao, Faheema Chaudhury, Angela Grammatas, Lefteris Grammatas, Teresa Huang, Sean Leo, Rebecca Saylor, Maneesh Yadav, Sheetal Jain, Anushka Ratnayake, Praveena Gummadam, Raina Telgemeier, Travis Kotzebue, Evan Hamilton, Christina Yunker, Anita Coulter, Tyler Null, and Catherine Kung, thank you for your unwavering support and granting me the right to bend your ear about this book. And to those unnamed supporters, I thank you, too—especially for forgiving my post-book forgetfulness.

For every person that's shared my work, sent me a note, purchased a card or print over the years, thank you many times over. Your support allows me to keep making art.

First Second

Library of Congress Control Number: 2016961589

Paperback ISBN: 978-1-62672-087-9
Hardcover ISBN: 978-1-62672-088-6

Our books may be purchased in bulk for promotional, educational, or business use.
Please contact your local bookseller or the Macmillan Corporate and Premium Sales Department
at (800) 221-7945 ext. 5442 or by e-mail at MacmillanSpecialMarkets@macmillan.com.

First edition 2017
Book design by Andrew Arnold
Printed in China by RR Donnelley Asia Printing Solutions Ltd.,
Dongguan City, Guangdong Province

Inked digitally in Flash, colored with Flash and
Photoshop on a Wacom Cintiq.

1 3 5 7 9 10 8 6 4 2